בס"ד
לד' הארץ ומלואה

This book belongs to :

_____

Please read it to me!

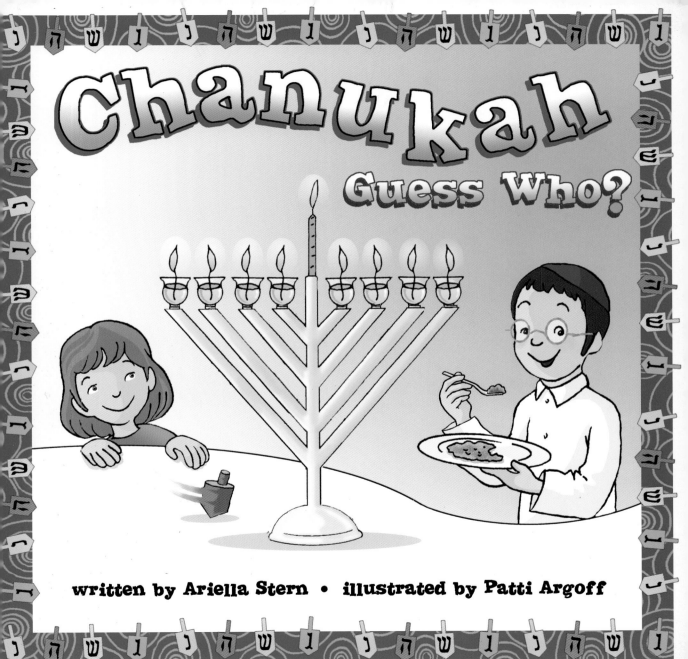

Chanukah
Guess Who?

written by Ariella Stern • illustrated by Patti Argoff

I'm in windows or by the door,
Never too high or on the floor.

With all my flames in one straight line,
My shamash and branches equal nine.

Who am I?

With wick and flame, I burn brightly,
Every night when people light me.

Who am I?

I am always helping others,

I'm like someone
with eight brothers.

Give me a twist, and make me spin,
Get a gimmel, and you will win!

I have more letters – shin, nun, hey –
Everyone takes a turn to play.

Some for tzedakah, some to lend,
Some to save, and some to spend.

Cooked or fried in oil that's hot,
We know you will eat a lot.

Yehudah led us in our fight,
To trust Hashem and do what's right.

I was hidden, pure and sealed,
Then I was searched for and revealed.

Chanukah Activities to Share...

- **Sit** in a circle with friends, and decide on a Chanukah song to sing. Let each person sing just one word of the song, and see how fast you can go!

- **Cut** construction paper into dreidel shapes and **decorate** with crayons or markers. **Tie** each dreidel to a piece of string or yarn and **hang** it from the ceiling. **Watch** those dreidels spin all Chanukah long!

- **Take** some index cards and **write** or **draw** a Chanukah object or character on each one. Whoever is "it" turns around while you tape one card on his back. That person needs to **ask** questions that help him guess what's written on the card: Am I big or small? Do I have four sides? Do people spin me? Once the person has guessed correctly, he chooses the next one to be "it," until everyone has had a turn. Whoever gets the right answer after asking the fewest questions, wins the game!

- **Think** of favors you can do for other people, like clearing the table, sharing your toys, or being quiet while they sleep. **Surprise** each person by doing that special favor as a Chanukah gift!

- **Read** *"Chanukah Guess Who?"* out loud to a whole group of friends and family, and see who knows the answers!

Happy Chanukah!

Glossary

Chanukah	Festival of Lights beginning on the 25th day of Kislev, celebrating the victory of the Jews over the Syrian Greeks and the miracle of the oil.
Chanukiyah	Candelabra
Gelt	Money
Gimmel	Hebrew letter corresponding to the 'g' sound. In dreidel games, the letter for "take all."
Hashem	G-d
Hey	Hebrew letter corresponding to the 'h' sound. In dreidel games, the letter for "take half."
Latkes	Potato pancakes
Maccabees	Heroes of the Chanukah story
Menorah	Candelabra
Nun	Hebrew letter corresponding to the 'n' sound. In dreidel games, the letter for "do nothing."
Pach HaShemen	Container of oil
Shamash	Helper candle that lights the others
Shemen Zayit	Olive oil
Shin	Hebrew letter corresponding to the 'sh' sound. In dreidel games, the letter for "add to the pot."
Sufganiyot	Doughnuts
Tzedakah	Charity

Chanukah Guess Who?

For my adorable boys -- Avinoam, Meir, and Ezzy --
who light up my life on Chanukah and every other day of the year! A.S.

First Edition - May 2012 / Iyar 5772
Copyright © 2012 by HACHAI PUBLISHING
ALL RIGHTS RESERVED

Editor: Devorah Leah Rosenfeld
Managing Editor: Yossi Leverton
Layout: Moshe Cohen

ISBN: 978-1929628-68-1
LCCN: 2012936453
Printed in China

HACHAI PUBLISHING
Brooklyn, New York
Tel: 718-633-0100 • Fax: 718-633-0103
www.hachai.com • info@hachai.com

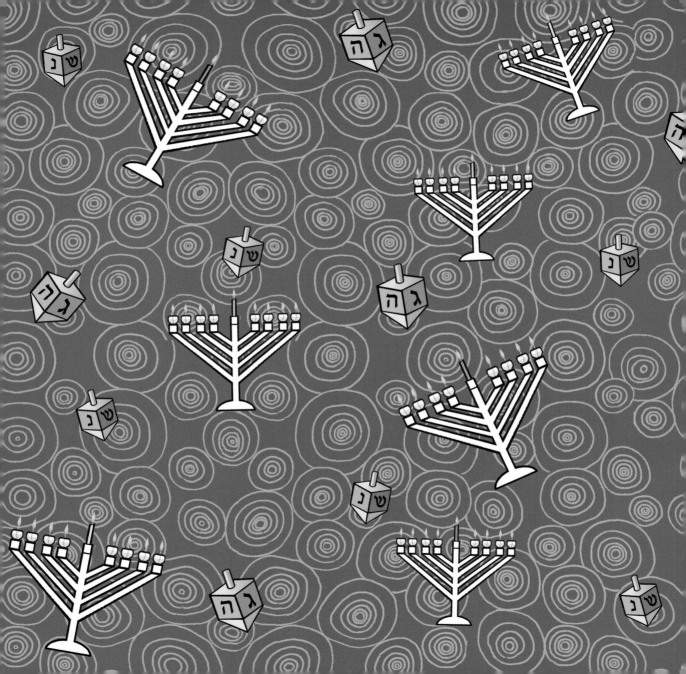